The Booger Genie

PRINCE OF PRANK

By N.E. Castle

Illustrated by
Bret Herholz and N.E. Castle

For my good friends.
May we always share laughter

To Joana Dion,

Read, &

Enjoy.

A. E. [signature]

TABLE OF CONTENTS

1. Snotty Little Prince 1

2. Prince of Prank 7

3. How Small You Will Be 15

4. A Tiny Bead 19

5. The Prince and the Peasant 23

6. Genies Aren't Real 29

7. Do What I Say 35

8. The Haunted Chair 41

9. The Principal's Office 49

10. Fickle Genie Magic 55

11. Good Deeds Shall Set You Free 63

12. Our Favorite Teacher 67

13. Miss Bellediddy 73

14. Learning To Wish 77

15. Dragon's Breath 83

16. Cut Off Your Nose 91

1.

Snotty Little Prince

A long time ago (805 years, to be exact), Garoth Castle stood atop a tall hill in England. Hundreds of torches lit its hallways. Dozens of statues danced in the flicker of flames. Their shadows moved like ghosts. Visitors were certain Garoth was haunted. Prince Loogar and his pranks had started that rumor.

Loogar was the Prince of Prank. (As the king's son, he was also known as the Prince of Garoth). He was eight years old and loved to play all sorts of pranks. He especially loved to frighten visitors. His pranks were the ghosts of Garoth. Yes, Garoth was haunted by Loogar.

Loogar's nanny, Miss Bellediddy, called him Loogie. The nickname fit him well because he was such a little snot. Eventually, Miss Bellediddy had suffered enough of Loogar's pranks. So one day she quit. Now the snotty little prince was free to do as he pleased. Without a nanny to stop him, Loogar was more prankful than ever.

Visitors ran screaming from ghostly wails. Grooms found holes in all of their pails. He put rocks in his mother's socks and pins in his father's pockets. Loogar's pranks spared no one.

Angered at the many pranks, servants mobbed the king. "We've been pranked enough!" they cried. The king did not know what to do.

He was a good man and a strong leader. He could fight any man and win any battle, but he could not make his prankish son behave.

Finally, the king turned to the wizard, Hendrick. He fell to his knees and begged for his help. "Please use your magic. You can cast spells to make Loogar behave. You can do this for me. Do this for all of us!"

"I will do what I can, my king," said the wizard. But he really did not know what to do. Hendrick spun around and disappeared down the hall, his long robes billowing behind him.

He found the prince in the kitchen. Loogar was pouring salt into a sugar bowl. Cooks were already sweeping up flour that he had scattered. Hendrick frowned, then raised the prince high in the air at the point of his wand.

"Put me down!" Loogar ordered. He waved his arms and legs frantically in the air.

"Sorry, my prince, but your father has asked that I keep you out of trouble. I see that I am already too late," said the wizard. Hendrick scowled. His face wrinkled up so tight that his snowy white eyebrows nearly hid his gray eyes. It was a very nasty scowl indeed.

Loogar squirmed and wriggled. He kicked at the wizard. "I can look after myself," he growled.

"Very well, but I have my orders from the king," said Hendrick. He then waved his wand. Loogar dropped to the floor with a thump. He quickly jumped up and brushed himself off. He glared at Hendrick, but the wizard just chuckled. Prince Loogar was a small, thin boy with sandy hair and freckles. An angry look from him was certainly not menacing.

"Off to your room then," said Hendrick. He pushed and pulled Loogar down a long corridor. The prince grumbled and fought all the way. Finally, they reached Loogar's very untidy room. "In you go to clean your room," said the wizard as  he pushed the prince inside. "It is quite a mess and should be neat."

"I DO NOT CLEAN MY ROOM!" shouted Loogar. "That is for the MAID to do!"

"Not today. The maid is away," said the wizard. "That means that the cleaning is up to you." Hendrick folded his arms across his chest. He blocked the doorway with his short, round body so the prince could not escape.

"Wave your wand to clean my room," Loogar ordered. "I am a prince. I do not do the work of servants!" He pushed against the wizard. But Hendrick did not budge.

"I could wave my wand," said the wizard. "But then you would have nothing to do but to cause more trouble. I will give you one hour to tidy up. In one hour, I will be back to see what progress you have made." He pushed Loogar back and closed the door. A quick tap of his wand locked the prince inside.

2.

Prince of Prank

Loogar did not do any cleaning. Instead he thought of a prank. He picked up a length of rope and a box of mice (he kept mice around for pranks). He punched a hole in the box and

looped the rope through it. Then he hung the box over his door. When he had finished, Loogar jumped up onto his bed to wait.

Hendrick returned in an hour as promised. As he opened the door, however, a dozen frightened mice tumbled onto his head.

They clawed at his eyes and his nose. One swung from his bottom lip. Another dropped right down the collar of his robes. He wriggled and jiggled a crazy dance. His wand sparked and zapped as he swatted the mice. It zapped chips and chunks out of the walls. One spark hit Loogar's pillow. Feathers flew everywhere.

Loogar laughed so hard that tears rolled down his cheeks. He held his belly as he laughed. He rolled on his bed and kicked his feet in the air.

"What is all that noise?" the queen called from down the hall. She was snobbish and proper. She hated loud noises in her very proper castle.

Hendrick quickly brushed away the last mouse. He

slipped his wand into his pocket and then faced the queen. "I am sorry, your highness. I am afraid the prince has played another of his pranks."

"Wizard! My husband has asked that you tend to my son. Do not turn him into a toad." The queen thrust her pointy nose in the air and looked down at the wizard. She really wasn't a very nice queen. (In fact, she could be quite mean).

The prince grinned. He jumped off his bed and hurried to his mother's side. The queen put her arm around him. She kissed the top of his head as Loogar snuggled up to her. He sneered at the wizard.

Suddenly, the queen yawned a big yawn. "I need one of your sleeping potions, wizard. Please bring it to my room. And do hurry." She walked away with Loogar under her arm.

"Yes, my queen," Hendrick sighed. He shook his head and grumbled. When they were out of sight, the prince slipped away from his mother. He ran straight to the wizard's laboratory.

Magical ingredients filled the laboratory. Lizard eyes and unicorn snot—really gross stuff—filled jars, bowls, and cups on a dozen shelves. Cauldrons of different sizes were stacked in the corner. Strange plants grew in pots on the floor.

Loogar grinned and pulled a bottle of pepper from his pocket. He dumped some into a jar marked "toad warts." He emptied the rest into a bowl of newt brains. As the wizard approached, the prince hid in the closet.

"I will show that spoiled little brat a thing or two," Hendrick muttered to himself. "But first, the queen must sleep." He tossed a few herbs and a pinch of spider hair into his cauldron. Then he added a large shake of newt brains to help the queen sleep.

Loogar giggled as he watched through a crack in the closet door. "You are no match for the Prince of Prank, wizard," he whispered. "I know what pepper does to your potions." He stayed hidden until Hendrick left the laboratory. Loogar then snuck down the hall toward his mother's room. He wanted to see his prank in action.

The queen was in her bed, propped up by a stack of pillows. She yawned and patted her mouth. She rolled her eyes as the wizard handed her

the potion. "Whatever took you so long?" she asked. Hendrick did not respond.

The queen took the cup and raised it to drink. But as the potion touched her lips, it exploded. It covered the queen in thick, black ooze—not a pretty sight. The ooze dripped from her nose and into her mouth as she screamed. She wiped it away with her hand. More ooze appeared.

"WIZARD! What have you done!" she yelled. Hendrick just stood there, frozen in horror. And then the sneezing started. She sneezed again and again. Each sneeze was louder than the last. Black ooze flew everywhere. "Make it… atchu!…STOP!" she screamed. Finally Hendrick waved his wand and her sneezing stopped. He waved it again and the black ooze disappeared.

By now the queen was frazzled. She glared at the wizard from under a mop of messy red curls.

"My queen, I am sorry," Hendrick apologized. "I cannot imagine what happened."

"You are an imbecile!" the queen shouted. "You had better find a new recipe."

"But I have given you this same potion a hundred times," he said. He took the cup and smelled it. "Pepper? There should not be pepper in this potion."

"A careless mistake!" the queen scolded.

"My queen, I do not keep pepper in my laboratory. It is dangerous to use in potions. This is Prince Loogar's doing. He has played one of his pranks," said Hendrick.

The queen stuck her nose in his face and glared at him. "Do not blame my son for your mistake! You are a terrible wizard! Maybe you will be a better cook. Go to work in the kitchen." She waved him off and turned away.

"But your majesty—!" the wizard said.

"Another word and you will be my butler," the queen said. She crossed her arms and thrust her nose in the air. (Very mean, indeed!)

"Yes, my queen," Hendrick sighed and left the room.

3.

How Small You Will Be

Loogar was outside the queen's bedroom. The prince was laughing so hard that tears rolled down his cheeks. He wrapped his arms around his belly as he laughed. He nearly doubled himself over.

The wizard reached out and grabbed a handful of Loogar's shirt. He yanked him close. "You think it is funny that I am punished for your pranks? I will give you something to laugh about. If the queen forbids me to use

my magic, then I will give it to you." Hendrick smacked his wand once on Loogar's head and cast a spell:

My magic I give you
A genie I make you
A slave in a pea
Is how small you will be
Made to serve a child like thee
Until good deeds done
Can set you free

Suddenly, Loogar began to shrink. He became so small that the wizard held him in the air with only

two fingers. Loogar kicked and flailed. He cursed and swore in a high-pitched tone. He sounded like an angry mouse. Now Hendrick was laughing. He held Loogar just out of reach of his nose.

"Perhaps this will teach you some manners," said the wizard. He grabbed a small, teardrop-shaped vase from a table and dropped the prince into it. Then he tapped the vase with his wand and it shrank to the size of a small pea.

"Goodbye, your snotty little highness," the wizard said to the pea. He flicked the pea across the room and it disappeared into a crack by the wall.

4.

A Tiny Bead

Charlie was seven when he took his first trip to see England's ancient castles. He loved castles, kings, and knights. He pictured himself as a king on a throne, laughing at court jesters. He imagined knights swinging swords as they rode through the courtyard.

The castle he now toured with his parents was in ruins. Much of the roof was gone and many of the walls had fallen to the ground. But Charlie found one room that was not ruined at all. The floors and walls were barely worn. The fireplace was lavishly carved. Over the door was a stone family crest. Outside, a steep, grassy slope rose to just a few feet below the windows. Charlie could see the whole valley.

His parents were looking at the wood carvings. Neither of them paid any attention to him. Charlie climbed up into the window. It had no glass. "Hey, Mom! Look at me!" he said as he teetered on the windowsill.

"Charlie! Get down from there!" they both shouted. His parents were scared, not knowing that the ground was only a few feet below the window.

"OK," Charlie said. But instead he pretended to lose his balance. He fell backward out of the window and screamed, "AHHHHH!" Then he was silent.

His mother yelled, "Charlie!" as both parents rushed toward the window. They found him sitting on the ground with a grin on his face.

"Charlie! You scared us half to death!" His father was angry. "Get back in here, right now."

Charlie laughed. He loved to prank his parents.

His father reached out and lifted him back through the window. "Please, don't EVER do that again."

"OK, Dad," Charlie said. He looked down at his shoes and fought a smile. He had gotten them that time! He knew his father liked his pranks. He said he had played pranks himself when he was a kid. Charlie could see Dad smiling even as he scolded him.

Charlie saw that one of his shoes was untied and bent down to tie it. It was then that he noticed a tiny brown bead stuck in a crack under the window. "Cool!" he whispered to himself. He would find a place for it in his model castle. Charlie found a stick and poked the bead up out of the crack.

It was not quite a round bead. It was shaped more like a teardrop. He dropped it into his pocket and continued exploring the castle.

His father had shown him how to use concrete and pebbles to build miniature walls and buildings. Charlie had built a model castle with walls eight inches high around six buildings. The castle's keep was the tallest. The keep was where the king and queen lived. When he got home, Charlie would add pebbles from the real castles to his miniature one.

5.

The Prince and the Peasant

After a week of exploring castles, it was time to return to school. Charlie was eager to tell his friends about the castles he had seen. He dumped the sock full of pebbles he

had collected onto his bed. The little brown bead rolled toward him. Charlie picked it up.

It was a strange bead. It had no place to tie a string. Beads always had a loop or a hole through them. This one had only a hole in one end. Charlie held it up close to get a better look. He sniffed at it. It smelled funny (probably 805 years of unwashed prince). Suddenly, the bead popped out of his fingers, right into his nose.

"Hey!" Charlie cried. "Get out of my nose!" He picked at the bead, but couldn't pull it out. Each time he tried to grab it, he pushed it further in. He pushed it so far up his nose that he could not see it when he looked at himself in the mirror. His nose started to

itch, so he scratched. Once, then twice he scratched. He squeezed and mashed his nose. He tried hard to pop the bead out. No luck—his nose still itched. Charlie rubbed his nose over and over.

Suddenly, his nose didn't itch anymore. It

burned—it swelled! He watched his nose swell before his eyes. Then he sneezed really hard. A flash of light blinded him and knocked him off his feet. When he opened his eyes, he was nose to nose with a freckle-faced boy his own age.

"Well, it is about time someone let me out of there! Where is that stupid wizard? He thinks he can cast a spell on me and lock me in a bottle? I will teach him a thing or two!" The strange boy turned to walk away but didn't go anywhere. A wisp of smoke seemed to tie him to Charlie's nose.

Charlie wiped his nose, but the smoke was still there. "Who are you?" Charlie asked.

"What do you mean, who am I?" the boy asked as he rolled his eyes. "I am PRINCE Loogar. Who are you, PEASANT?"

"I'm Charlie and...I think..." Charlie walked over to the mirror. "Oh, my gosh, you are!"

"What?" said Loogar as he turned to look in the mirror. He saw that a part of himself seemed stuck in Charlie's nose. "Ugh! You dreadful peasant! What did you do?"

"I didn't do anything," Charlie cried, as he mashed his nose. "That bead jumped into my nose. That bead was you! Get out of my nose!" He pulled at the wisp of smoke.

"Do not blame ME for this. YOU did this!" Loogar pushed against Charlie's cheeks. He tried to pull himself free. Finally he collapsed and hung upside down from Charlie's nose, a great, big, dangling booger.

Charlie shook his head. The prince flopped back and forth.

"You MUST pull me out," Loogar groaned. "I cannot stay in the nose of a peasant." He lifted his head, then flopped back down again.

"Maybe I can help," Charlie said. He grabbed Loogar by the shoulders and tugged. He pulled the prince away from his nose as far as he could. But it wasn't very far.

Charlie had another idea. "We'll use the door," he said.

He pushed Loogar out of the room, then closed the door and latched it shut. Charlie was now inside the room while the prince was outside. Charlie backed away. He felt the tug at his nose like a great big booger. He backed away from the door ten feet. The bead stayed lodged in his nose. It did not move. Suddenly, the wisp of smoke yanked at his nose. It yanked so hard that Charlie flew forward. He smashed his face against the door.

"Ow! That's not funny!" Charlie yelled. Loogar yanked again. Again, Charlie smashed his face. Loogar roared with laughter. Charlie rubbed his nose and pulled the door open. Loogar was rolling around in the air, gripping himself where his belly should have been. But Loogar had no belly. His body ended below his chest. That was where the wisp of smoke began, snaking its way to Charlie's nose.

"You look like you have a great big booger hanging out of your nose!" cried Loogar as he continued to laugh.

Charlie turned bright red. "At least I'm not the booger. You're the booger!"

"I am not a booger," said the prince. "I am a genie!"

"Your name is Loogie and you're stuck in my nose. You're a booger genie. Get back in your bottle!" yelled Charlie.

Loogar's eyes opened wide. Suddenly he was sucked back into Charlie's nose. "Ow!" Charlie yelled. It felt like a baseball was being shoved into his nose. Then the prince was gone. Charlie looked in the mirror, expecting his nose to be at least twice its original size. But to his surprise, he looked the same as he always had.

6.

Genies Aren't Real

"Charlie!" his mother called. "You're going to be late for school."

"I'll be down in a minute," he yelled back. He ran to the bathroom for a pair of tweezers. He grasped the bead and yanked at it. It wouldn't budge. The bead was lodged firmly in his nose.

"Charlie!" his mother called again.

"Coming!" he replied. Loogar would have to wait.

Charlie's nose tickled during the whole ride to school. He pushed and poked at his nose, but it didn't help. It was really hard not to scratch or rub his nose. If he scratched or rubbed too much, he knew the genie would come out again, because rubbing his nose rubbed the genie's bottle.

"Are you all right?" his mother asked.

"Uh-huh," he said, as he rubbed his nose once really hard. Finally they stopped in front of the school. Charlie grabbed his books. He then jumped out of the car and said goodbye. He ran into the school and straight to the bathroom. He locked himself in a toilet stall.

Charlie rubbed his nose until the genie burst out and floated in front of him. "I am a PRINCE. You do not lock me up in a PEASANT nose," Loogar scolded. He folded his arms across his chest and scowled at Charlie.

"Sorry," Charlie said. "You have to stay in your bottle."

"Why would I stay in that dreadful bottle?" Loogar asked.

"Because you're not real," Charlie said.

"But of course I am real. I am a prince!" Loogar sneered.

"You're a genie, and genies don't exist," Charlie said. He rubbed his nose, which hurt from having Loogar burst out of it.

"Nonsense!" Loogar shouted. "My father has a genie in his castle. Tildor is his name. Tildor did far worse things to earn his punishment than I."

"Being a genie is punishment?" Charlie asked. "But you can do magic. How is that punishment?"

"Genies are magical creatures that have been imprisoned as slaves. They can only use magic for their masters," Loogar said. "A master does not always wish for good magic. But a genie must do as his master wishes."

"So you can only do magic for me?" Charlie asked.

"You are NOT my master. I do not HAVE a master. I am a PRINCE," Loogar said snobbishly. "I was not a magical creature. I should not be a genie. Tildor was an evil wizard. He had magic. Hendrick cast a spell on him and made him a genie."

"Wow! Did he put Tildor into a tiny bottle like yours?" Charlie asked. "Is he Tildor's master?"

"No, Tildor's bottle is tall and slender. My father is Tildor's master. He forces him to use his magic against Pawklin Castle. That is Tildor's punishment—Pawklin is his home," Loogar explained with a sneer.

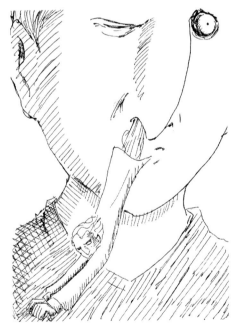

"Does a genie have only one master? What if someone else rubs the bottle?" Charlie asked.

"The genie may appear for another if he chooses," Loogar huffed. "But a genie has only one master. One master is quite enough."

"So what happens if I die?" Charlie asked.

"Then I will sleep until another peasant rubs my bottle," Loogar sighed.

Charlie heard the bathroom door open. "Quick, get back in my nose!" he whispered. Before he could protest, Loogar was sucked back into Charlie's nose. Charlie winced—you would too if a genie flew into your nose.

7.

Do What I Say

A couple of boys walked in. They talked for a few minutes. Charlie listened while Loogar tickled his nose.

After the boys left, Charlie scratched

vigorously. He didn't even stop as Loogar flew out of his nose. The genie floated angrily in front of him. "What did you do THAT for?" Loogar demanded. "Do not send me back into your slimy nose!" He reached out to slap Charlie across the face. Charlie cringed, but Loogar's fingertip just brushed the tip of his nose. Charlie was surprised.

"What? How dare you move! Hold STILL, peasant!" Loogar ordered.

He swung his other hand to slap Charlie. But that slap, like the first, only grazed the tip of Charlie's nose. "This will NOT do," Loogar said. He slapped at Charlie again and again with no success. Each time, his fingertips just missed the tip of Charlie's nose.

The prince then grabbed Charlie's hair. He yanked as hard as he could, but Charlie's hair just slipped through his fingers. Loogar tried again, but he still could not pull Charlie's hair.

Charlie laughed. "I get it. You're not allowed to hurt your master."

"You may have awakened me, but you are NOT my master. I'll have you whipped for suggesting it, peasant!" Loogar said.

He folded his arms and turned his nose upward.

Charlie laughed again. "You can't do anything to me. You have to do what I say. I'm your master," he taunted.

"Where is that wizard, Hendrick? Where is my castle?" he demanded.

"I don't know where the wizard is, but your castle is back in England. I went there with my parents.

"You went to my castle? You? A peasant? Ridiculous!" Loogar sneered. "My father would NEVER allow peasants in my castle."

A group of boys flung the door open and piled noisily into the bathroom. Loogar quickly covered Charlie's mouth as he held a finger to his own lips. Charlie said nothing.

After several minutes, the group left the bathroom.

"Thank you for not sending me back into that dreadful bottle," Loogar said. "Now, tell me why my father allowed you into my castle."

"Your father wasn't at your castle," Charlie said. "No one was there but tourists."

"Tourists?" Loogar's face wrinkled up.

"Yes, tourists. Your castle is a museum," Charlie said.

"WHAT!" Loogar exclaimed. "Why would my castle be a museum?"

"It's old and ruined," Charlie said. "The guide said it was almost a thousand years old."

Loogar was stunned. "Nonsense," he whispered. A tear formed in the corner of his eye. He looked scared. "My castle is only one hundred and sixty years old. My great-great-grandfather built Garoth."

Charlie shook his head. "A thousand years old."

Loogar shuddered and started to cry. He slumped back and hung upside down from Charlie's nose.

"Sorry, Loogie, but it's not so bad," Charlie said as he pulled Loogar up by his hand.

"Not so bad? I was to be king!" he moaned. "I was to marry a beautiful princess when I grew up. Now I am a booger in the nose of a peasant. I have lost my parents and my kingdom because of that stupid wizard!"

Suddenly, the bathroom door opened again. "Charlie, are you in here?" a boy asked.

"Get back in my nose," Charlie whispered.

8.

The Haunted Chair

"Hi, Tom. I'm in here," Charlie said.

"Katie's wearing pink. You know pink is for pranks," Tom said. "She wants to prank Miss Turner. We need your help. Do you have any ideas?"

Charlie thought of a prank he had played on his father. "Yes, I have an idea."

"Cool!" Tom said. "Let's go find Katie."

Katie waited for them outside of their classroom. She was dressed head to toe in pink. She always wore at least one pink thing. But wearing all pink meant she wanted to cause some trouble.

"I've been trying to think of a prank to play on Miss Turner. Please tell me you have some ideas!" Katie said.

"We can make her chair follow her around the room," Charlie offered.

"Okay. How do we do that?" Katie asked.

Charlie pulled a roll of duct tape from his backpack.

Katie shrugged. "I bet you a milkshake it won't work," she said. She flipped her blonde hair back and walked into the classroom.

Charlie cut two lengths of string from a spool in Miss Turner's drawer. He tied one end

of each string to a strip of duct tape. He tied the other ends to the arms of her chair. Then he placed the strips of tape sticky-side-up on the seat. They pushed the chair under her desk then sat in their seats.

The classroom began to fill with students. Finally, Miss Turner arrived.

"She'll see the tape," Tom whispered.

"Not if we distract her," Charlie whispered back.

Tom nodded. "Hi, Miss Turner!" he said.

"Do we have a test today?" Charlie asked.

"No," Miss Turner said. "We don't have a test today. We just got back from vacation." Miss Turner looked at them as she walked to her desk. Their plan to distract her was working.

"I would be ready for a test. I did my homework," Charlie said.

"That's very good," Miss Turner replied.

"I studied last night," Tom said. "If you gave us a test, I would do really well." The other students groaned. They did not want a test.

"I'm sure you would do well. But there won't be a test today," Miss Turner replied.

"Miss Turner, will we have homework tonight?" Katie asked.

Miss Turner arrived at her desk. She looked at Katie as she pulled out her chair. Then she started to look down.

Charlie acted fast. He smacked Katie's shoulder as hard as he could. "OW!" Katie screamed.

"Of course we have homework!" Charlie said. "We ALWAYS have homework."

Miss Turner looked sharply at him. "Charlie! Don't hit girls," she scolded. She gave him a stern look and plopped into her chair. She sat right on the duct tape. She never noticed it.

Charlie, Tom, and Katie covered their mouths. They tried hard not to laugh.

Miss Turner opened her textbook and looked at the class. She wriggled in her chair. That would help the tape stick, Charlie thought.

"Open your books to Chapter 5," Miss Turner said. She spent several minutes talking about math. Finally she stood up.

The class broke into snorts, giggles, and belly laughs. The tape had stuck! Miss Turner's chair rolled behind her. It followed her to the board. The children's laughter grew louder.

"Class, pay attention," she said. She wrote on the board. She did not notice the chair.

Their laughter quieted to snickering.

Charlie, Tom, and Katie grinned at each other. Their prank was a success!

Suddenly, the chair rolled into Miss Turner like it had been pushed. It bumped her so hard it knocked her feet out from under her. She sat down in the seat with a thump. The chair took off across the room, spinning like a teacup ride at a carnival.

The students laughed out loud.

"WHAT'S GOING ON?" Miss Turner screamed. She hugged her knees to her chest.

Then the chair stopped. Miss Turner jumped up and hurried away from it. The string tightened and the chair followed.

The students laughed harder.

"Why are you laughing?" she demanded. "This isn't funny! My chair is haunted!"

She stopped to look over her shoulder and saw the strings. She took a step forward. The chair followed.

"Who did this?" she asked. She glared at her students. Her face turned redder and redder.

Loogar tickled Charlie's nose fiercely. Charlie began to sneeze again and again.

Miss Turner looked over at them. "Charlie, Tom, and Katie! Go to the principal's office right now! Leave that tape here." She pointed to the roll of duct tape hidden in Tom's shirt.

Charlie saw the folded end of the tape flap like it was waving at him. "Loogie!" he whispered angrily. Loogar had made Charlie sneeze so Miss Turner would look at them and see the tape.

9.

The Principal's Office

The principal scowled at the three students entering his office. "I see you've gotten yourself into trouble again."

"Hi, Dad," Charlie said. "We didn't mean to get caught."

"Then you should not have done whatever you did," his father replied.

Charlie's father had become principal at his school this

year. Now Charlie could not hide anything from his parents.

"What DID you do?" his father asked.

"We played a prank on Miss Turner," Katie replied. "We stuck tape to her butt and got her chair to follow her around."

"Hmmm. Charlie's idea, I'll bet," he said. "He pulled that one on me. But Miss Turner hates to be pranked. It's not nice to prank someone who doesn't like to be pranked. You realize this means detention."

"Yes, sir," they replied together. Their shoulders slouched and they hung their heads.

"You and I will talk about this later, Charlie. Now go back to class. I'll see you all later for detention."

They nodded, sighed, and left his office.

Katie turned to Tom. "Nice going, Tom. You got us in trouble. You were supposed to hide the tape."

"If Charlie hadn't sneezed a zillion times, she wouldn't have looked at us and seen the tape," Tom said.

Charlie's nose tickled and he bit his lip.

Detention finally ended late in the afternoon. Charlie's father drove him home.

"Charlie, you have to stop playing pranks now that I'm the principal. People will think I go easy on you just because you're my son. That means I have to give you twice the punishment I would the other kids. I don't want to do that, so I need you to stop. I'm going to have to ground you to your room for a week," he said.

"Yes, Dad." Charlie didn't argue. He knew that if he did, a week would quickly become two weeks.

They arrived home and Charlie went straight to his room. He rubbed his nose and Loogar burst out.

"Why did you get us in trouble?" Charlie asked.

"Your prank was boring," Loogar yawned. "I made it better. Then I played a prank on you. I am the Prince of Prank!"

"We made everyone laugh without your help," Charlie said.

"They were just being nice," Loogar sneered.

Charlie heard footsteps on the stairs. "Quick! Back in my nose!" he whispered.

Charlie's mother opened the door. She always checked on him when he was grounded. She gave him chores if she was angry with him.

"Come down and help me set the table for dinner," she said.

Charlie sighed and followed her. His mother was angry.

Charlie gathered plates from the cabinet and placed them at each chair. As he turned to get forks, one of the plates jumped off the table onto the carpet.

"Loogie! Stop it!" Charlie whispered.

Another plate jumped and skidded across the floor into the kitchen.

"Charlie! Did you just throw one of my dishes?"

"No, Mom. It just slipped out of my fingers. I tried to catch it."

"Please be more careful," she said.

"Yes, Mom."

He put the plates back on the table. They started moving, ready to jump.

"Loogie, stop throwing plates! You'll break my mother's dishes," Charlie ordered.

The dishes stopped moving.

Charlie finished setting the table and sat down. His father arrived and sat across from him.

"Smells like spaghetti!" His father breathed deeply and grinned. He rubbed his belly hungrily.

Charlie's mother entered the room with a big platter of spaghetti covered in sauce and meatballs.

"That is a thing of beauty!" Charlie's father exclaimed.

"Thank you!" His mother smiled and set the platter in front of them.

Charlie filled his plate then cut eagerly into a meatball.

"Charlie, your father told me what you did to Miss Turner today," his mother said. "You can't keep playing practical jokes. Eventually, one of your jokes might hurt someone."

"I know, Mom. I won't do it again," Charlie said.

Loogar tickled his nose. He wanted Charlie to know he was laughing.

10.

Fickle Genie Magic

After dinner Charlie returned to his room. He rubbed his nose as hard as he could. Loogar had tickled him all through dinner.

"Stop tickling my nose!" Charlie said.

"Do NOT send me back into that bottle," Loogar demanded. "I will NOT stay in that bottle."

"Well, your bottle is stuck in MY nose," Charlie said.

"So pull it out," Loogar ordered.

"I tried, but I can't," Charlie replied.

"Well then, we will just have to cut off your nose," the prince said matter-of-factly.

"What! I'm not cutting off my nose!" He felt his nose and added, "I like my nose where it is."

"Well I do NOT like being stuck in your nose," Loogar huffed.

"Look, I haven't been able to pull you out of my nose. Maybe we're stuck together. It would be better if we were friends. If you would stop getting me in trouble, we could be friends."

"A prince does not need friends. I want you to cut off your nose," Loogar demanded.

"I'm not cutting off my nose," Charlie insisted. "Now help me with my homework. It's history about England."

"You want me to tell you about a home that I will never see again?" Loogar asked sadly.

"I know you miss home. It looked like a really cool place. I wish I could see what it was like when you lived there," Charlie said.

Instantly, the walls of Charlie's bedroom disappeared. They were replaced by walls of plaster and stone.

"What—? Where are we?" Charlie asked.

"I am home!" Loogar exclaimed. "This is Garoth Castle!"

Charlie looked around at statues and colorful paintings. Torches burned in the corners. He recognized the room where he had found Loogar's bottle.  But it was no longer ancient and ruined.

Suddenly, laughter echoed through the room. Charlie and Loogar turned to look.

"Hendrick!" Loogar yelled.

"I never imagined how my spell would be carried out." Hendrick was laughing so hard there were tears in his eyes. He pointed at Charlie. "You must be trouble, just like Prince Loogar."

"I'm not trouble. I'm a good kid," Charlie said.

"If that were true, then my prince would not be lodged in your nose," the wizard laughed.

"Wait until my father hears about this," Loogar said. "Fa—!" Instantly, his mouth disappeared.

"Have you not learned your lesson?" Hendrick said. "No, you are a spoiled brat. You still have a lot to learn."

He gave Loogar his mouth back. Loogar did not yell again.

"Why are you still dressed as a wizard? Did my mother not send you to be a cook?" Loogar asked.

"My dear prince, I turned you into a genie just moments ago," replied Hendrick.

"Then how is it I have spent years in a bottle?"

The wizard scratched his long white beard as he pondered. "Your master made a wish, perhaps. Yes! Genie magic is the most fickle of all magical arts," the wizard chuckled. "Its primary rule is simply that all magic must serve the genie's master. So MUCH is possible. But this magic has limits, too. For instance, you cannot grant a wish for riches. If you try, nothing will happen."

Loogar huffed. "I would not try. He is a peasant. He does not need riches."

Hendrick turned to Charlie. "You must phrase your wishes carefully or you may not get what you want. But your princely friend should not tell you how to craft your wishes. The magic of wishes works best if the wish is truly yours. Learning to use genie magic is really quite fun."

"This isn't fun. You're mean!" Charlie said. "When I get into trouble, my parents ground me. They don't turn me into a booger and lock

me up in someone's nose."

"Ah! But what I have done is the same," the wizard said. "Your booger friend IS grounded. And until he changes his ways, he will STAY grounded in his bottle."

"Do you mean that Loogie could come home?" Charlie asked.

The wizard shrugged. "Perhaps."

"How?" Charlie asked.

"By waving his wand," Loogar replied angrily. "Set me free now and I will spare your life, wizard."

Hendrick shook his head. "I cast the spell, but only you can break it. Do good deeds, not pranks. You must right your wrongs if you are to be free."

"Argh! I demand that you bring me home, now!" Loogar ordered.

Loogar launched himself at the wizard. The wisp of smoke pulled sharply at Charlie's nose. Charlie nearly fell on his face.

Hendrick shook his head and chuckled. Then he waved his wand.

Suddenly, they were back in Charlie's bedroom. Hendrick was gone. The castle was gone, too.

11.

Good Deeds Shall Set You Free

"I was home! I was back in Garoth! How did that happen?" Loogar asked.

"I don't know," Charlie said. "The wizard mentioned a wish. I think I wished to see your castle."

"Yes! You did!" Loogar said. "Perhaps you could wish me to go home. You could even wish me to not be a genie anymore."

"OK. I wish you were not a genie," Charlie said.

Loogar remained a wisp of smoke.

"Why did that not work?" Loogar asked. "Say it again."

"I wish you were free," Charlie said.

Still, nothing happened.

Charlie sighed. "I don't know why that didn't work. I wish we could ask the wizard."

Instantly, they were back in the castle. But this time the castle walls were old and crumbled.

"I see you have still not learned your lesson," said the wizard. "How many years has it been? Hmmm...eight hundred and five." The wizard laughed and shook his head. He was much frailer than he had been, and his flowing white beard and hair had been trimmed short.

Loogar looked around at the crumbled walls. "Where are we?"

"We are in Garoth Castle," the wizard replied. "But it is many years since I saw you and your friend. Am I to understand that you have been in your bottle all this time? No one has let you out before this?" The wizard smiled cruelly. "It must have been torturous."

"Why are you still here?" asked Loogar.

"This is where I work," said the wizard. "I stayed to serve your father. When your mother bore a new son, I stayed to serve him when he became king. I've served every king who descended from your father and ascended to the Garoth throne. Even as wizardry went out of style and was replaced by science, I stayed. Garoth Castle is my home. I know of no other home."

"Why can't I wish Loogie to be free?" Charlie asked.

"Only good deeds done can set him free," said the wizard. Hendrick then repeated a portion of the spell he had cast. "The spell demands that Loogar do good deeds. Only then might he break the spell and be free. Now, be gone!" The wizard waved his wand.

They appeared midair in Charlie's bedroom and then fell to the floor. Charlie landed on top of Loogar. He flattened the prince.

Charlie sat up. Loogar flopped under his nose.

"Watch where you land, peasant," he groaned.

12.

Our Favorite Teacher

The next morning, Charlie met Tom and Katie. "I got grounded for the week," he said. "What did your parents do to you?"

"I got a week. No more trouble for me for a few days," Katie said. Her pink sneakers were the only bit of pink that she wore. She would not prank in so little pink.

"Your parents are easy. I got grounded for two weeks," Tom whined.

Miss Turner walked in. The three friends were instantly quiet. They watched her as she walked to her desk. Miss Turner glared at them. She checked her chair before she sat down. She looked around at the rest of her students. Her eyes became moist. She looked very sad.

Finally, Miss Turner cleared her throat. "This will be my last week of teaching here at this school," she said. Her voice trembled.

The class hushed.

"Why are you leaving?" asked little Jenny Lynn in the back of the class. She was Miss Turner's favorite. "Will you be back?"

Miss Turner shook her head. A tear rolled out of the corner of her eye. "I believe Mr. Sampson will substitute until you get a new teacher," she

said. The class groaned at the mention of Mr. Sampson. He was the most boring substitute teacher EVER.

Jenny Lynn climbed up on her chair. She was little, but standing on her chair, she seemed huge.

"This is YOUR fault!" she screamed at Charlie, Tom, and Katie. "If you weren't so mean to Miss Turner, she wouldn't be leaving."

"Jennie Lynn, please sit back down," Miss Turner said sternly.

"But, Miss Turner—," she protested.

"In your seat. It's not nice for you to yell at other children like that," Miss Turner said.

Jenny Lynn sniffled, then climbed down from her chair. She shot a last angry look at Charlie, Tom, and Katie and plopped back into her seat. Charlie saw that the rest of the children now looked angrily in their direction.

"Miss Turner, are you really leaving because of us?" Katie asked.

"Katie, I have a class to teach," Miss Turner scolded. "You can see me during the break if you like."

"Yes, ma'am," Katie mumbled. She folded her arms and slumped down in her seat.

Miss Turner directed the class to open their books. She started to teach them as though nothing were different. But she was going to leave. Miss Turner was their favorite teacher ever. Everything was different!

"Jenny Lynn is just being a brat. Miss Turner likes us," Tom whispered to Katie and Charlie.

"But we should ask her," Charlie whispered back. "I don't want her to leave because of us."

When the class ended, Charlie, Tom, and Katie stayed in their seats. Miss Turner finished wiping the board. She turned back to her desk and saw the three of them still sitting.

"Miss Turner?" Charlie said.

She frowned at them. "What can I do for you?" she snapped.

"Are you leaving because of the pranks we played?" Katie asked.

"You don't look very happy about leaving," Tom said.

"If you're leaving because of our pranks, we're sorry," Charlie said. Miss Turner looked surprised. Her expression softened a little.

"We were just having fun," Katie added. "We thought we made you laugh."

Miss Turner smiled sadly. "Thank you, children. But your pranks do not make me laugh. It hurts my feelings when people laugh at me."

"Sorry," Charlie said. "My dad laughs when I play pranks on him."

"You play pranks on your father?" she asked.

"All the time. He pranks me back, too. But I promise we won't play any more pranks if you'll stay," Charlie said.

She laughed. "I'd like to stay. Your apology means a lot to me. I like being your teacher. But I don't like the pranks."

"We promise, then. No more pranks," Charlie said.

Tom and Katie agreed. "No more pranks— EVER!"

13.

Learning to Wish

When Charlie got home, he ran up to his room. Loogar had tickled his nose all day. Now he scratched it really hard until Loogar whooshed out.

The prince looked worried. He did not look snobbish at all. "Your teacher was going to leave because you played pranks on her. Is that why Miss Bellediddy left me? She did not like my pranks?"

"Who is Miss Bellediddy?" Charlie asked.

"She was my nanny, but she left. I miss her," Loogar said. "Did she leave because of my pranks?"

"Maybe. I wish we could ask her," Charlie said.

Suddenly, they were in front of a giant cave. Loogar was confused. "This is the ogre's cave. Why are we at the ogre's cave?"

"Ogre?" Charlie asked.

Then a faint cry for help sounded from within the cave. "Oh no! The ogre has Miss Bellediddy!" Loogar exclaimed. "He'll feed her to the dragon if we do not save her!"

"Save her? Aren't ogres big, ugly, and mean?" Charlie asked. He was very frightened.

"Yes, we have to go in and find her!" Loogar urged.

"Sure, if I were invisible," Charlie said.

"Yes! Invisible! Good idea!" Loogar said. He waved his hand and Charlie disappeared from view.

Charlie looked down at his feet. They were gone. He kicked a rock and it rolled away from him. "Cool! I'm invisible! But what about you? I can still see you."

"I can fix that," Loogar said. He snapped his fingers over his head but nothing happened. "Oh, I know what is wrong. A genie can only do magic for his master. Sadly, that is you, peasant. You must wish for me to be invisible."

"Okay, I wish you were invisible," Charlie said.

But Loogar still floated before his eyes. "I believe it does not work because the magic would be used on me," Loogar groaned.

"But we are here for you to ask Miss Bellediddy why she left. I was able to wish that for you," Charlie said.

"I believe you wished that WE could ask her," Loogar said. "The magic was for you."

"So, I wish that WE were invisible," Charlie said. But still Loogar remained visible before him.

Loogar looked at his hands and sighed. "I do not need to be invisible for you to be invisible."

Loogar said. "But since I am lodged in your nose, I do have to go wherever you wish to go."

"Ugh! Learning to wish is hard," Charlie groaned. "If we can't make you invisible, then I guess you'll have to hide in my nose. I'll have to find Miss Bellediddy by myself."

"Do not get us killed," Loogar warned and disappeared into Charlie's invisible nose.

14.

Miss Bellediddy

The ogre was nowhere to be seen inside the cave. Charlie tiptoed down a long tunnel. It was bright with the fire of torches. They cast an eerie glow and Charlie jumped as shadows danced along the wall. He was sure that the ogre would appear at any second. He didn't feel invisible in this very creepy cave and he was scared.

The tunnel led to a large cavern. He found Miss Bellediddy there hunched in the corner of a wooden cage. Her face was buried in her hands. Charlie heard her crying.

Loogar tickled and Charlie rubbed his nose. The prince appeared in a puff of smoke. Since Charlie was invisible, he seemed to be alone.

"Miss Bellediddy, are you OK?" Loogar asked as he floated outside the cage.

She raised her head. "My prince! Why are you here? And why do you seem a wisp of smoke?"

"I am a genie," he explained. "I am here to help you."

"But why are you a genie?" she asked.

"I played a prank on the wizard and made him angry. He turned me into a genie."

"Did I not tell you that your pranks would get you into trouble?" she said.

"Did you leave because of my pranks?" Loogar asked. "Did I hurt your feelings?"

Miss Bellediddy pointed to her hair. It was purple and orange and very untidy. "You turned my hair this horrible color and painted a moustache and beard on me. You embarrassed me. It took me days to remove the paint from my face. The cooks now call me 'Grape Head'."

"I am very sorry," Loogar said.

"Where is your master?" Miss Bellediddy asked Loogar. "Surely you must have a master if you are able to leave your bottle."

Before Loogar could answer, loud footfalls sounded within the tunnel.

"You must hide, quickly!" Miss Bellediddy said.

"I am a genie. I do not need to hide," Loogar said. "I will use magic to get us out of here."

"Your magic will only benefit your master. It is meant for no other," Miss Bellediddy said. "That is the genie rule."

"Argh! What good is my magic, then?"

The footfalls grew louder. They were coming closer. "I don't think we have time to look for an exit," Charlie said. "We'll have to block his path."

Miss Bellediddy drew a sharp breath. "Who is that?"

"That is my peasant master, Charlie," Loogar said. He waved his hand at the empty air and Charlie appeared.

"Loogar, block the ogre's path," Charlie said. "Maybe you can make the ceiling cave in."

"Good idea," he said. Loogar then began to make cutting motions in the air with his hands.

Huge boulders broke away from the ceiling and fell down to block the ogre's path.

"That will keep him away from us for a little while," Loogar said.

"Nicely done, my prince," Miss

Belledíddy said. "Now, may I ask why you are stuck in Charlie's nose?"

"Hendrick says it is because he plays pranks, like me," Loogar replied. "The wizard said I have to do good deeds to be set free."

"I believe that will be difficult for you, my prince. But you have done a good deed by coming to save me. Thank you, my prince." She curtsied and Loogar smiled smugly.

"Charlie, your clothing is quite unusual. Where are you from?" Miss Belledíddy asked.

"I'm from New York," Charlie said. "New York State, not New York City."

"I know of York, but not of a New York City or New York State," Miss Belledíddy said.

"That's because it doesn't exist yet. Columbus won't sail across the Atlantic for another few hundred years, I guess," Charlie said.

"You came from the future? But how did you get here?"

"Just by accident, really. I made a wish and here we are," Charlie said.

"Wow! A genie granted a wish to send you across time. I did not think that such magic was possible."

"Yeah, it's pretty cool. Loogar grants all of my wishes," Charlie said. "Loogie, could you open the lock on Miss Belledidddy's cage?"

"Of course, peasant." Loogar smiled and waved his hand. The lock popped open.

"Wonderful!" Miss Belledidddy jumped up excitedly. She was eager to be free.

"We can't go out the way we came in. Is there another way out of here?" Charlie asked.

"I do not know. A bird flies from over there every day." Miss Belledidddy pointed toward another tunnel at the back of the cavern. "Perhaps there is another exit."

15.

Dragon's Breath

Charlie and Loogar led the way into the tunnel. Miss Bellediddy huddled close behind. The tunnel was dark, but they found a small

hole in the wall that let in a tiny shaft of sunlight. The hole was only large enough for Loogar to squeeze through.

Charlie put his face up to the hole and Loogar poked his head outside. The prince looked down the face of a cliff. A river flowed two hundred feet below them. Loogar wriggled back out of the hole.

"I can widen this opening, but we are at the top of a cliff. I do not know how we can get down," Loogar said. He traced a circle in the air with his finger. Then he punched the air in the middle of that circle. A large rock broke from the wall and fell to the water below. It left a round doorway in the cave wall.

"That is a long way down," Miss Bellediddy said when she saw the cliff. "We will die if we jump. Charlie, you can wish yourself out of here. But I will have to stay here with the ogre. Loogar's magic cannot help me. It can only help you."

"I have an idea," Charlie said. "I can make a wish. I wish I could fly us out of here."

Charlie expected an airplane or maybe a glider to appear. But this was not the age of man-made flight. This was the age of magic and mystical creatures. Instantly, Charlie became an enormous dragon. He cowered under the low ceiling of the cave.

Charlie arched his long neck to look around at himself. He saw wings and a huge dragon body. "Oh, wow! This is awesome!" Charlie roared with fiery breath. "When I fly, I should be able to carry Miss Bellediddy."

Loogar jumped away from Charlie's

breath just in time. He was still attached to Charlie's nose and he was dangerously close to being singed.

"Please be careful with your breath, peasant!" Loogar snapped.

"I think that you will need a larger hole," Miss Bellediddy suggested.

"You're right. Loogie, can you make a hole big enough for me to get out?" Charlie asked.

Loogar grinned. "Watch this, peasant." He cut at the wall of the cave with his hands and a rock the size of a house fell away into the water below. The cool air rushed in.

"Thanks, Loogie! Miss Bellediddy, climb onto my shoulders," Charlie roared. He hunched his massive shoulders down so that she could climb up.

Suddenly, footfalls sounded again. The ogre had broken through the rubble. He was coming for them!

"Be quick! Hurry!" Charlie urged. Miss Bellediddy struggled and pulled herself up.

Charlie leaped out into the air, just out of the ogre's reach. The ogre teetered at the edge of the cliff, then plunged into the water below. Charlie flew above the spot where the ogre had fallen, but the creature did not surface. It appeared the ogre had drowned.

"I think you killed the ogre!" Miss Bellediddy cheered.

"That may be true—but we have company," Charlie called.

Miss Bellediddy looked behind them. Another dragon bore down upon them. It blasted fire at them, catching Charlie's tail.

"Yeow!" Charlie cried. He plunged toward the water and leveled out across its surface. He dipped his tail in the water then landed by the trees.

"Get off, quickly!" Charlie roared. Miss Bellediddy jumped off and ran for cover. Charlie launched himself skyward just as the dragon plunged toward him. He banked to the right and narrowly escaped another blast of fire.

Just then, the other dragon dove toward the water. Charlie looked and saw the ogre splashing around. He was alive, but he could not swim. The dragon swooped in and snatched up his friend, then flew out of sight, clutching the ogre tightly.

"Yay! We did it, Loogie!" Charlie crowed. He circled around, then glided back to where he had left Miss Bellediddy. "I wish I was myself again," Charlie said, and suddenly he was a boy again. His trousers were slightly singed from the breath of the other dragon.

"I am a hero! Now the wizard can turn me back into a prince!" Loogar cheered. "Miss Bellediddy, will you come back to the castle to be my nanny? I promise I will not play any more pranks."

"Perhaps," Miss Bellediddy said.

"I will be home as soon as I am free," Loogar said.

"Will you be going back through time?" Miss Bellediddy asked. "Does Garoth Castle still stand where you are going?"

"Garoth is in ruins," Charlie said. "I live eight hundred and five years in the future. Loogie's father and mother are no longer alive."

"Amazing!" she exclaimed. "Genie magic is truly impressive! Boys, may I hug you both

before you return home? You have been so kind to save me from the ogre." She wrapped her arms around them. Loogar was squished in the middle. As she held them, Miss Bellediddy slipped a tall, slender bottle into Charlie's pocket—Tildor's bottle. Charlie never noticed.

16.

Cut Off Your Nose

"Wish us to the wizard," Loogar told Charlie eagerly.

Charlie made the wish. Suddenly, they stood before the frail, aged wizard in the crumbling old castle. He was trimming the hedges.

"I am a hero, wizard. Can you free me now?" Loogar demanded.

Hendrick laughed. "If you are not free, then the spell is not broken. A few good deeds do not outweigh a thousand bad ones."

"But we saved Miss Bellediddy from the ogre!" Charlie said.

"Ah yes, I do remember the day she returned to the castle. She said that she owed her life to Loogar. Your father was very proud."

Loogar smiled. "My father has never been proud of me before," he said.

"How many good deeds do we have to do before Loogie is free?" Charlie asked.

"I cast his spell in anger," said the wizard. "I did not think of details. Perhaps one more deed will set him free. Perhaps he must do as many good deeds as he has done bad ones. I do not know."

"But this is so unfair!" Loogar argued.

"Perhaps, but as you can see, I have work to do." He pointed to the hedges. "Goodbye for now." Hendrick waved

his wand and once again the boys appeared midair in Charlie's bedroom. Charlie twisted to avoid landing on Loogar. Tildor's bottle popped out of his pocket and bounced under his bed, out of sight.

Charlie stood up and rubbed his sore bottom. "We're stuck like this?" he asked. "How many pranks have you played?"

Loogar flopped down and hung from Charlie's nose. "I was the PRINCE of Prank," he groaned. "We will have to cut off your nose."